Tommy
The Timid Turtle

Written by Neva Swartz

Illustrated by Larry Steinbauer

Dedicated with love to Bruce & Linda, Brian & Karen
and all my Grands

Neva Swartz

Mayhaven Publishing

P O Box 557
Mahomet, IL 61853 USA
All rights reserved.
Copyright © 2004: Neva Swartz
Copyright © 2004 Illustrations by Larry Steinbauer
First Edition/First Printing 2004 1 2 3 4 5 6 7 8 9 10
ISBN 1878044-75-3

Library of Congress Control Number: 2004106859

Printed in Canada

Tommy was a very timid turtle.

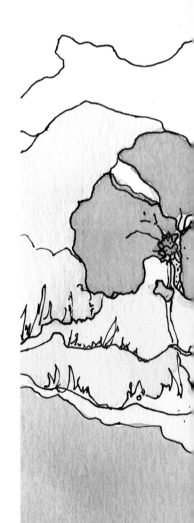

Freddy Fox wanted Tommy to come out to play, but Tommy was shy.

Snappy Squirrel wanted Tommy
to come out to play leap frog, but
Tommy was bashful.

Henrietta Hen wanted
Tommy to come out to play
hide-and-seek, but Tommy
was afraid.

Doxie Dog wanted Tommy to come out to play follow-the-leader, but Tommy was cautious.

Drucilla Duck wanted
Tommy to come out to swim,
but Tommy was scared.

Bobby Bird wanted
Tommy to come out to
play ring-around-the
rosy, but Tommy was
timorous.

Randy Raccoon wanted Tommy
to come out to play ball, but
Tommy was fearful.

Timothy Turkey wanted Tommy to come
out to play London-bridge-is-falling-down,
but Tommy was alarmed.

Rodney Rooster wanted
Tommy to come out and hunt
worms, but Tommy lacked
courage.

Clementine Cat wanted Tommy to come out to run, but Tommy lacked confidence.

Sammy Sun wanted Tommy to come out to see his shadow, but Tommy was insecure.

So Sammy Sun
shone brighter.

And brighter

And brighter

Suddenly,
Tommy put
out one foot.

And another foot.

And then a third foot.

And a
fourth foot.

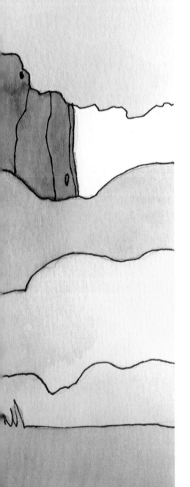

And finally, his head.

Sammy Sun was beaming.

And all the animals were happy, and he had so much fun playing with his friends, now Tommy isn't timid anymore.